Princess Ponies

A Unicorn Adventure!

For Iyla, who inspired these adventures

With special thanks to Julie Sykes

Bloomsbury Publishing, London, New Delhi, New York and Sydney

First published in Great Britain in June 2013 by Bloomsbury Publishing Plc
50 Bedford Square, London WC1B 3DP

A CIP catalogue record for this book is available from the British Library

ISBN 978 1 4088 2730 7

Typeset by Hewer Text UK Ltd, Edinburgh
Printed and bound in Great Britain by CPI Group (UK) Ltd, Croydon CR0 4YY

1 3 5 7 9 10 8 6 4 2

www.bloomsbury.com
www.ChloeRyder.com

Princess Ponies U

A Unicorn Adventure!

CHLOE RYDER

BLOOMSBURY

LONDON   NEW DELHI   NEW YORK   SYDNEY

The Pony

Queen
Moonshine

Princess
Crystal

Princess
Cloud

Princess
Stardust

Princess
Honey

Royal Family

King
Firestar

Prince
Jet

Prince
Comet

Prince
Storm

Chevalia

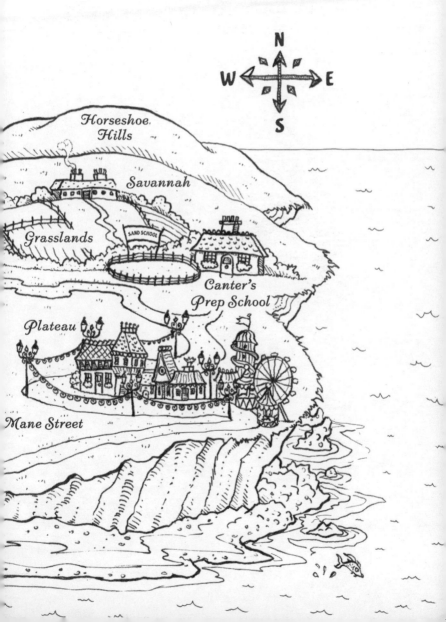

N
W E
S

Horseshoe Hills

Savannah

Grasslands

SAND SCHOOL

Canter's Prep School

Plateau

Mane Street

Early one morning, just before dawn, two ponies stood in an ancient court-yard, looking sadly at a bare stone wall.

'In all my life this wall has never been empty. I can't believe that the horse-shoes have been taken – and just before Midsummer Day too,' said the stallion.

He was a handsome animal – a copper-coloured pony, with strong legs and bright eyes, dressed in a royal red sash.

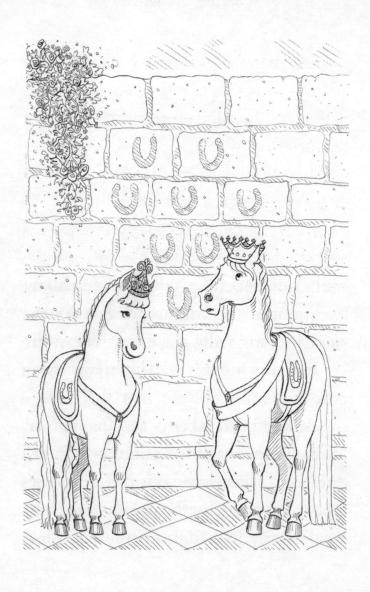

The mare was a dainty yet majestic palomino with a golden coat and a pure white tail that fell to the ground like a waterfall.

She whinnied softly. 'We have so little time to find them all.'

With growing sadness the two ponies watched the night fade away and the sun rise. When the first ray of sunlight spread into the courtyard it lit up the wall, showing the imprints where the golden horseshoes should have been hanging.

'Midsummer Day is the longest day of the year,' said the stallion quietly. 'It's the time when our ancient horseshoes must renew their magical energy. If the horseshoes are still missing in eight days, then by nightfall on the eighth day, their magic will fade and our beautiful island will be no more.'

Sighing heavily, he touched his nose to his Queen's.

'Only a miracle can save us now,' he said.

The Queen dipped her head regally, the diamonds on her crown sparkling in the early morning light.

'Have faith,' she said gently. 'I sense that a miracle is coming.'

Chapter 1

Pippa woke with sunlight warming her face and the sound of singing in her ears. The music reminded her of her big sister, Miranda, who often sang in the mornings. Miranda was mostly out of tune though, unlike the beautiful voices Pippa could hear now. Curious, she got out of bed.

'Stardust, are you awake?'

Princess Stardust's straw duvet was crumpled as if she'd got up in a hurry. A wave of homesickness hit Pippa as she stared around the empty room. Annoying as Miranda was, she missed her – and Mum and her little brother, Jack. Would they be missing Pippa too?

Four days ago Pippa and her family had been on a seaside holiday when two giant seahorses had taken her to the enchanted island of Chevalia, a world inhabited by talking ponies. Pippa had learnt that Chevalia was in terrible danger. The eight golden horseshoes that gave the island life had been stolen from the Whispering Wall, an ancient courtyard wall in Stableside Castle. If the horseshoes weren't hanging back on the wall in time for Midsummer Day, their magical energy couldn't be renewed by the Midsummer sun and Chevalia would fade away. To Pippa's amazement, she had been asked to find the missing horseshoes. Along with her new best friend, a Royal Pony called Princess Stardust, she'd managed to find four of them, but Midsummer was in three days' time and there were still four horseshoes to find.

As Pippa got up she remembered something important – Chevalia existed in a magical bubble. No time would pass in her world while she was on the island, meaning that none of her family would miss her. Pippa's homesickness vanished immediately.

She skipped over to the window to see where the singing was coming from.

Princess Stardust's bedroom was in the smallest turret of the Castle, topped with a pink flag, and it had a marvellous view. Pippa glanced at the sea sparkling in the distance before her eyes were drawn to the courtyard below.

'It's the Royal Court,' she breathed.

All the ponies of the Royal Court were gathered together, with the Princesses and Princes at the front. Their colourful sashes and jewelled tiaras shimmered in the morning sun. Crystal, Stardust's bossy eldest sister, was conducting the singing with a riding crop and the music made Pippa want to dance. When she had first arrived on Chevalia Pippa had been so shy, but now she was starting to feel as if she belonged here and she couldn't wait to join them.

Pippa quickly put on the new outfit that had magically appeared overnight especially for her – a denim skirt, a stripy T-shirt, leggings and a horseshoe-patterned top – then she hurried down the turret's spiral ramp.

'Excuse me,' she whispered as she edged her way to the front of the court-yard. The Royal Ponies smiled as they parted to let her through. 'Thanks,' she said.

Princess Honey was singing next to Stardust, tapping the ground in time to the music with a sparkly pink hoof. She was very pretty, with a shiny, straw-berry chestnut coat, but she couldn't

quite reach the higher notes and her voice kept squeaking.

'You sound like a rusty stable door,' Stardust said, laughing at her.

Honey hung her head.

'Hi, Stardust. Hi, Honey,' Pippa whispered, squeezing between them. 'What's going on?'

'We're rehearsing for the Royal Concert,' Stardust replied. 'We always hold it on Midsummer Day, to give thanks for Chevalia and the magical horse-shoes. But Honey won't be allowed to sing if she keeps on making that racket.' She playfully nudged her older sister.

Honey's brown eyes filled with tears. 'You're so mean!' she said. Pushing past Stardust, she trotted out of the courtyard.

'There isn't going to be a concert if we don't find the horseshoes,' said Pippa. 'But before we carry on searching for them you'd better find Honey and say sorry for hurting her feelings.'

Stardust was surprised. 'I was only teasing. I didn't mean to upset her – I forgot how much she wanted to sing the solo.'

Stardust was anxious to make it up to her sister so together they sneaked out of the Royal Courtyard.

Once outside, she whinnied to Pippa, 'Get on my back.'

Pippa jumped on to Stardust's snowy white back and they cantered off to look for Honey.

'There she is,' Pippa said, pointing,

as they left the Castle over the draw-
bridge.

'She's heading for the Grasslands,'
Stardust said, galloping after her.

Leaning forward like a racing jockey,
Pippa buried her fingers in Stardust's
mane. She galloped so fast that the air
rushed at Pippa's face, making her eyes
water and her hair stream out behind
her in dark, curly ribbons.

Honey didn't stop at the Grasslands
but galloped on across the Savannah.

'Where's she going?' Pippa shouted.

'I don't know.' Stardust sounded
worried. 'This is the way to the Cloud
Forest but she can't be going there,
surely.'

'Why not?'

Stardust's stride faltered slightly. 'Because it's haunted.'

Pippa's fingers tightened on Stardust's mane, knowing that if Honey entered the haunted forest she and Stardust would have to follow her.

'Faster,' Pippa urged.

Stardust lunged forward.

'Honey, wait!' called Pippa. 'Stardust has something to say to you.'

They were almost at the edge of the Cloud Forest when Stardust finally caught up with Honey.

'I'm sorry,' Stardust panted. Her sides were heaving and Pippa slid from her back to give her a chance to get her breath back. 'I didn't mean to hurt your feelings.'

'I can't sing either,' Pippa confided. 'I'm useless at it and I get so shy I go bright red.'

'You, shy!' Stardust and Honey exclaimed together.

Pippa nodded. 'I'm very shy about lots of things but Mum says if you pretend to be confident then everyone will think you are.'

Stardust was impressed. 'That's great

advice! I never guessed that you were shy about anything.'

'So where were you going, Honey?' Pippa asked. 'Have you got a secret hideaway?'

Honey blushed and shuffled her hooves. 'Sort of,' she admitted. 'If I tell you the truth you won't believe me.'

'Why won't we believe you?' asked Pippa.

'It's a secret, so you have to promise not to tell anyone,' Honey said. 'I was going to see my friend Goldie. She lives in the Cloud Forest.'

'No one lives in the Cloud Forest,' said Stardust.

Honey took a deep breath. 'She's a unicorn.'

'A unicorn?' Pippa breathed, her eyes as round as plates. 'Unicorns are real?'

'Oh, please!' Stardust snorted with laughter, until she noticed that Pippa was glaring at her. 'There's no such thing as a unicorn,' she said. 'Unicorns are make-believe — they only exist in bedtime stories for foals. Besides, you wouldn't dare to go into the Cloud Forest – everyone knows it's haunted.'

Just then a beautiful noise drifted towards them. As they stood and listened, Pippa wished her ears could prick up to detect sounds like Stardust and Honey's.

'What's that?' she whispered.

'It's the ghosts!' neighed Stardust. 'Hop on my back, Pippa. We should get out of here.'

Now it was Honey's turn to laugh. 'Oh, please!' she parroted. 'There's no such thing as a ghost. That's the sound of the unicorns' song.'

'It's beautiful,' Pippa said, feeling herself soothed as if by a lullaby.

'It's amazing!' said Honey. 'But I've never heard them sing together like that. We must find Goldie and see what's happening.'

'No!' Stardust dug her hooves into the ground. 'You can't go into the Cloud Forest. It's far too scary.'

'I'm not scared,' Honey said stubbornly.

'Wait!' Pippa said, as Stardust started to trot away. 'If most ponies are too afraid to enter the Cloud Forest, doesn't that make it a brilliant place to hide a horseshoe?'

Stardust stopped and stared at Pippa. 'You're right,' she agreed.

'Let's go then,' Pippa said bravely. 'We can look for horseshoes and singing unicorns at the same time.'

Chapter 2

Stardust hesitated, but Pippa and Honey were already stepping towards the line of trees that marked the entrance to the Cloud Forest. A thick mist swirled around the trees, making it impossible to see more than a tail's length ahead. Pippa took tiny steps, screwing up her eyes to try to see her way.

'Watch out,' Honey called, tossing her red brown mane.

Pippa stopped. A thick, green bundle of vines, coarse like old rope, snaked down from an enormous tree and blocked their way.

'Are they poisonous?' she asked.

'No, just heavy,' Honey said, pushing them back with her nose as Pippa and Stardust joined her. 'The first time I came here the vines took me by surprise and I walked straight into them. You should have seen the bruise I got – it hurt for ages.'

'They're very easy to miss in this mist,' said Pippa.

Pippa walked past the vines, holding them out of the way, then let them go when Stardust and Honey were clear.

'Vines like that could knock out an

elephant,' Pippa giggled, watching them swing back across the path like a giant pendulum.

'What's an elephant?' Honey and Stardust asked together.

'Well,' Pippa began, searching for the right words. 'Elephants are much bigger than ponies, and have thick, grey skin and long trunks that extend from their faces and which they use to drink up water.'

'Now *that* sounds like a creature for a bedtime story!' said Honey.

'Not if you want a good night's sleep!' Stardust laughed. 'They sound scary.'

As they walked deeper into the forest the mist closed in behind them and seemed to swallow them up. Pippa stared around nervously, half expecting a dinosaur to lumber out of the oversized trees. The ground was springy with a thick carpet of leaves. A huge, green plant grew everywhere, with leaves like aeroplane wings and vibrant red flowers.

'It's like an ancient forest,' she whispered.

'It is an ancient forest,' Honey whispered back.

'It smells wonderful.' Stardust stopped to take a deep breath.

'Listen.' Pippa tilted her head to one side. She could still hear voices singing in the distance but now there was a new burbling noise competing with it. 'What is that?' she asked.

The sound was familiar but she couldn't work it out.

Stardust tossed her head. 'I can hear it too.'

'It's a stream,' said Honey. 'The forest has lots of brooks and ponds. They're partly why everything grows so well here.'

The ground was becoming spongier as they followed the sound of the beautiful voices. Water oozed through Pippa's sandals, making her toes wet. Stardust daintily flicked her hooves, showering Pippa's legs with sparkling droplets of moisture. Pippa couldn't help giggling, and the noise sounded out of place in the impressive forest, like laughing out loud in a library.

'That was cold!' she said.

'Sorry.' Stardust hung back so that she didn't splash Pippa any more.

The ground grew boggier until, finally, they reached a brook. It was small enough to jump. Honey went first, clearing it easily, then turned back and called for the others to join her.

Before Pippa could go anywhere though, something buzzed above her head, producing a draught of air that lifted her hair and tickled her neck.

'Eek!' Stardust whinnied, swinging around.

Her eyes were wide with fright and she reared up, her brown hooves pawing at the air.

Pippa's mouth fell open. Ducking down on the leafy ground, she covered her head with her arms. A bird-sized creature darted overhead, red flames shooting from its mouth.

'Help! A dragon!' neighed Stardust.

Honey almost fell over her pink hooves laughing. 'A *dragonfly*,' she said, calmly correcting her. 'Stand still and

stop panicking. Dragonflies won't hurt you, though accidents can happen if you get in their way.'

Pippa's heart thundered like a machine. It was all very well Honey telling them to stand still, but knowing what to do and actually doing it were two very different things. She slowly stood up and stroked Stardust's trembling neck. Stardust whinnied softly. The dragonfly circled above them then, in a whirl of electric-blue wings, it spun away.

Pippa exhaled in relief. 'Wow!'

Chevalia was full of magical surprises. Yesterday she'd met talking horseflies and now here was this amazing fire-breathing dragonfly. What would she see next?

The music was growing louder. It made Pippa think of tinkling raindrops and colourful rainbows sparkling in the sunshine. She hurried on, eager to discover where it was coming from. The mist began to thin out. In places it hovered around her waist so that she

felt like she was swimming through it.
Pippa was so wrapped up in the magical
surroundings and the sweet melody of
the music that she almost missed the
dog crossing the path ahead. It was only
when Honey shouted out that she
looked up.

'Goldie!' Honey called.

The creature bucked, kicking out its
back legs, and Pippa realised it wasn't a
dog at all. It looked more like a tiny
pony, rose-tinted brown with a flowing
blonde tail.

Honey took off, galloping after her.

'Wait for us!' shouted Pippa and
Stardust.

Pippa's heart hammered against her
ribs as they hurtled into the trees after

Honey. What if they lost her? How would they ever find their way back out of this enchanted Cloud Forest? Fallen branches snapped under her feet and damp leaves were kicked up in her face. Pippa pushed herself to run harder, determined not to be left behind.

After a long chase, she and Stardust burst into a small clearing carpeted with mossy flowers, their golden petals shining like the rising sun. Honey stood at the base of a tree, its trunk twisted with age. She was speaking softly to someone and Pippa looked around to see who it was.

A low branch stretched, like a twiggy arm, from the tree into the clearing. Perched gracefully in the middle of the branch was the strange, rose-tinted brown pony. Its silky tail flowed down like a waterfall. It had soft brown eyes and a blonde mane. Pippa couldn't help staring at the creature's forehead. She blinked but it was still there. The creature definitely had a gold, spiralled horn in the middle of its forehead. Pippa's breath caught in her throat.

'A real unicorn,' she whispered, blinking to check that she wasn't imagining the beautiful creature.

'This is Goldie,' Honey said, turning round to face them.

'Hello,' Goldie said, her voice like the tinkle of bells.

'Hello,' Stardust said, curtsying.

Pippa curtsied on trembling legs but her voice was stuck in her throat and she couldn't speak. The unicorn was like a smaller, more delicate copy of Honey! Not wanting to be caught staring, Pippa lowered her eyes.

'Hello, Stardust. Hello, Pippa,' said

32

Goldie. 'Honey's just been telling me all about you.'

'Hello,' Pippa said, finally finding her voice.

The unicorn was much smaller than she had expected – not that Pippa had ever expected to meet a real unicorn. But then she had never expected to meet giant seahorses or talking ponies either. On Chevalia it seemed that just about anything was possible.

Pippa was entranced by the tiny unicorn, her golden horn shining brightly in the dappled light of the forest. Pippa's gazed flicked to Honey. There was no denying it. Honey and Goldie were almost identical.

'I'm so glad you came today,' Goldie continued in her sweet, tinkling voice. 'Strange things have been happening here in the Cloud Forest. This morning when we sang our waking song, a tree sang back to us.'

Honey was puzzled. 'A tree sang back to you?' she asked.

Goldie nodded, dipping her head. 'The others are still singing to it.'

'A singing tree,' Pippa wondered aloud. It sounded like magic – the sort of magic that might come from a very special horseshoe. 'Where's this tree?' she asked. 'Can you take us there?'

Goldie looked uncertain. 'I could, but it's in the very heart of the forest. And my family might be surprised to see you – they've never seen real, live girls before. Are you sure you want to make the journey?'

'Yes,' said Pippa. Turning to Stardust, she explained her thinking about the magical horseshoe.

Stardust whinnied with excitement. 'We must look at this tree!' she exclaimed. 'Please can you take us there?'

Goldie gracefully sprang down from the tree. 'Yes, follow me.'

Chapter 3

The deeper they went into the Cloud Forest, the spookier it became. Sometimes the mist swirled around them so thickly that it was impossible for Pippa to see her own feet. Shivering a little, she wondered what the Royal Ponies thought about their sudden departure from singing practice. Would they come looking for them if they failed to return?

The ancient trees were enormous and branches brushed against her like gigantic spiderwebs. But with Goldie leading the way, her horn shining brightly in the gloom, Pippa's courage soon flooded back.

After a while she heard the roar of water. The trees thinned and they came to a huge, raging river of muddy, brown water. Goldie stopped on the squelchy bank and waited for everyone to catch up.

'We're not going to cross that, are we?' Stardust asked nervously.

'It's quite safe if you know how.' Goldie tried to reassure them. 'Follow me closely and only put your hooves where I put mine.'

Stardust nudged Pippa's arm and asked, 'Would you like to ride on my back?'

For a second Pippa was almost tempted, but it wasn't fair on Stardust to make her carry an extra weight. She shook her head. 'Thanks, but I don't mind walking.'

'This way,' Goldie said, moving upstream.

She stopped at a slender tree branch that had fallen into the river. Pippa eyed it uncertainly. The branch only reached halfway across the river.

'There are stepping stones from the middle to the other side,' Goldie said, guessing at her concern. She gracefully jumped up on to the branch and walked to the middle. 'Follow me,' she called.

Honey went first but Stardust made Pippa go next.

'So I can jump in and rescue you if you slip and fall in,' she said, smiling.

'What if *you* fall in?' asked Pippa.

'I won't.'

'Then I won't either,' Pippa said.

She took a deep breath then stepped up on to the tree branch. It was slippery with spray from the river. Pippa hesitated. Then she remembered a PE lesson she'd had at school in which the teacher had asked them to walk along a low beam in the gym. 'Find something to look at straight ahead,' the teacher had told them. 'Focus on that and don't look down.'

With the teacher's words ringing in her ears, Pippa inched her way along the branch until she was balanced over the middle of the river. The next part was even scarier because Goldie was expecting her to step down on to a rock

in the river. The water roared past with an angry hiss.

'It's easy,' called Honey, who had already reached the second stone.

Carefully, Pippa stepped off the branch and on to the first stepping stone. She wobbled as she landed but, using her arms, she managed to regain her balance. After that it was simple. The stepping stones were bigger than she'd thought and she quickly made it to the other side.

'That was fun,' Stardust said, jumping on to the bank beside her.

The mist was starting to thin out even more. Pippa stared around her, marvelling at the beauty of the ancient woodland and the huge trees soaring above her. As Goldie weaved through the forest, the singing grew louder. It rang in Pippa's ears and made her want to dance and skip. Goldie led them on, until she finally reached the biggest tree Pippa had ever seen. It had a tall, redwood trunk that was rutted and grooved like a muddy track. Its branches stretched stiffly out with a fan of whispery, green leaves. Circling the tree was a herd of tiny unicorns, their golden horns gleaming in the darkness. Their heads were held high and they were singing at the top of their melodious voices.

Pippa gulped back tears. The music was so special it made her want to cry.

'Listen,' Stardust whinnied softly. 'Can you hear that?'

Pippa nodded. 'The tree's singing back to the unicorns.'

Every line the unicorns sang, the tree sang it back to them like an echo.

'Isn't it marvellous?' Stardust's face glowed with excitement.

The unicorns clearly loved it too. They sang on, their voices high and pure.

Scrunching up her eyes, Pippa peered up the huge, red tree trunk. She was sure one of the golden horseshoes must be hidden in the branches, but where was it?

Suddenly she noticed that one of the singing unicorns was watching the

ponies with enormous eyes. Pippa
smiled, and the unicorn snorted and
looked away. A few seconds later it
looked again. Pippa stood very still.
The unicorn stared at her then, breaking the circle, it cautiously trotted
over. Pippa caught her breath. In the
same way that Goldie and Honey were
very similar, so were Stardust and this
unicorn. The unicorn planted her
hooves in the ground, swishing her
snow-white tail as she stared up at
Stardust.

'You're funny,' she said.

'Excuse me!' spluttered Stardust.

'Did your horn fall off? You look
really silly without it.'

Pippa swallowed a chuckle. That was

just the sort of untactful thing that Stardust often blurted out without meaning to. But Stardust wasn't laughing. Hanging her head, she pawed at the ground.

'I don't look silly, do I?' she whispered to Pippa.

'Of course not,' Pippa replied.

'I'm sorry,' the unicorn said quickly. 'My name's Misty and I'm always putting my hoof in it. I didn't mean to hurt your feelings.'

But Stardust was too upset to listen and began trotting away.

'Come back,' Pippa said, hurrying after her. 'Just because you don't look exactly like someone else that doesn't mean you're funny or strange. It's not nice to tease others about the way they look, whether they're people, ponies or unicorns. But I'm sure Misty didn't mean to be unkind. We all do things without thinking about the consequences. You know, like laughing at someone when they don't sing very well.'

A red flush crept up Stardust's snowy neck. 'I understand,' she said.

Pippa wrapped her arms around Stardust and gave her a big hug. As she pulled away, she noticed something glinting in the branches above her. Pippa squinted at the redwood tree. Was she imagining things or . . . ?

'Stardust,' she said, her voice squeaking with excitement, 'what do you see up there?'

Stardust looked up to where Pippa was pointing and gasped. 'A horseshoe!'

'It's the fifth one,' Pippa said happily.

The horseshoe was resting on the edge of a huge, untidy nest, jammed between a branch and the tree's giant trunk. It was a long way up. Pippa shivered. She was scared of heights but

she'd been learning to overcome her
fear during the hunt for Chevalia's
missing horseshoes. The tree looked
like a straightforward one to climb.
There were lots of handholds on its
rough trunk and, if she stood on Stardust's back, she could easily reach the
lowest branch.

'What have you seen?' Misty asked, joining them.

Pippa quickly explained about the missing horseshoes and how the island of Chevalia couldn't survive if they weren't returned to the ancient court-yard wall in time for Midsummer.

'I see,' Misty said doubtfully. 'But you'll have to be careful.'

'Why?' asked Stardust.

'That's not just any old nest. That nest belongs to a dragonfly.'

Pippa and Stardust stared at each other in horror.

'What do we do now?' asked Stardust.

'There's only one thing we can do,' Pippa said. 'We need the horseshoe so I'll have to climb up and get it.'

Chapter 4

For once Princess Stardust was lost for words.

'That's far too dangerous,' she whinnied at last.

'We don't have a choice,' Pippa said firmly. 'Neither you nor Honey can climb up there.'

'Definitely not,' Honey agreed, anxiously glancing at her sparkly pink hoof gloss.

Worry lines creased Stardust's snow-white face. 'Are you sure you want to do this?'

'Yes,' said Pippa. The giant seahorses had brought her to Chevalia to save the island. She was the only human ever to go there. Many of the island ponies had been suspicious of her at first, but now they trusted her and were counting on her – she couldn't let them down.

Misty raised a hoof to show that the unicorns should pause for a moment in their circling of the tree.

Quickly, before her nerves got the better of her and she changed her mind, Pippa beckoned Stardust closer. The dragonfly nest looked empty. If she was quick she could retrieve the horseshoe before the dragonfly returned.

'Please stand here, under this branch,' Pippa said.

Reluctantly, Stardust stepped forward. 'You don't have to do this –' she began.

'I do,' Pippa said. She made an effort to sound cheerful but knowing that Stardust was scared for her somehow made her feel braver.

Swinging herself on to the Princess Pony's back, she carefully stood up on it. Once she'd got her balance she was able to reach up and grab the lowest branch of the tree. The rough bark bit into her hands but, ignoring the discomfort, Pippa gripped it tightly as she began to climb up the tree trunk. Before

long she had straddled the branch in the same way she would a pony. Relief made her feel light-headed.

'Easy-peasy lemon squeezy,' she called down to Stardust.

'Lemon squeezy? Is that something humans drink?' Stardust asked.

'No,' Pippa said emphatically.

'It must be what those elephants drink,' Stardust explained to Honey.

Pippa was too out of breath to explain that it was just a rhyme.

Pippa looked above her. There were only a few more branches to go before she reached the dragonfly nest. She tried to ignore the prickle of fear that was giving her goosebumps. Pulling herself up so that she was standing on the branch, she reached up for the next one. Pippa climbed slowly, checking each branch could hold her weight before relying on it. Every time she went higher she worked out the best places to put her feet before she moved them.

Far below, Stardust and Honey were whinnying encouraging words. And, softly in the background, the unicorns sang as they continued to circle the tree. Their lyrical voices gave Pippa courage and, as the tree echoed their beautiful music, Pippa climbed faster and higher, until she was sitting on the branch directly below the dragonfly's nest. She was out of breath and, even though she was itching to carry on climbing, she made herself sit still until her heartbeat had slowed.

'Are you all right?' called Stardust.

'Yes, thanks,' Pippa shouted, glancing down at her friend.

Immediately she wished she hadn't looked down. The ground was much further away than she'd expected. Stardust, Honey, Misty, Goldie and the circle of unicorns were toy size. No wonder their singing seemed to be fading in comparison to the tree, which was loudly singing back to them. There was a sick feeling in Pippa's stomach and she became dizzy. Unable to tear her eyes away from the ground, she realised the unicorns were all staring up at her. It was very unnerving. All at once it hit Pippa that she hadn't asked the unicorn herd's permission to climb their tree and it was too late to ask now. She wondered if the unicorns realised that it was the horseshoe magic that was making the tree sing back to them. Nervously she wondered what they would say when she removed the horse-shoe and the tree stopped singing.

'Well, I'd better get on with it.' Pippa took a deep breath and huffed it out in a sigh. Now that she'd stopped she'd lost the urge to climb any higher. And she wasn't keen on climbing back down either. She was tempted to just sit there for a little while.

'No – I can do this,' she said firmly.

Quickly, before she changed her mind, she reached up for the last branch and hauled herself on to it. The nest, huge and untidy, reminded Pippa of the rooks' nests high in the city trees at home. It was filled with four large, green, oval eggs. Pippa caught a glimpse of herself in the shimmering surface of the largest. The eggs were beautiful and seemed totally out of place in the scruffy nest. Pippa's heart lifted as her eyes were drawn to a sparkle of gold.

'The missing horseshoe!'

It was wedged between the largest egg and the side of the nest. As she leaned forward, the horseshoe was just within her grasp. Wrapping one arm around the branch, Pippa reached out with her free hand . . . and froze.

'Oh no!' she gasped.

The eggs were moving. She watched

in horror as long, jagged cracks ran across the eggs' smooth shells. The cracks grew and the eggs began to rock then to split open. A chunk of shell the size of a marble landed on Pippa's hand.

'Ouch!'

The shell was hot! Pippa quickly flicked it away. A long, slim leg emerged from one of the eggs. It was soon followed by a second leg. The legs waved in the air. A loud snap startled Pippa and she clung tightly on to the branch as the egg cracked in two. A round head with two huge eyes looked around in surprise. More legs were appearing from the other eggs. Soon there were four heads and eight startled eyes peering out of the nest. The baby dragonflies kicked away the broken shells and slowly unfolded their delicate, tissue-like wings.

'Oh!' Pippa sighed, mesmerised by their beauty.

Each dragonfly had a different hue to its silvery body and wings. The largest was turquoise, the second largest was red, the third had a purple hue and the smallest was pink. The colours sparkled in the weak rays of sunlight that had managed to filter through the thick canopy of trees.

Without meaning to, Pippa had leaned forward for a better view. A tiny roar, followed by a jet of orangey-red

flames, made her jump back in alarm. Snatching at some leaves, Pippa only just stopped herself from falling. Now all four dragonflies were hissing fire. Pippa's nose twitched as she breathed in the sharp smell of smoke. To her left a cluster of leaves was smouldering.

'Thank goodness for the mist,' Pippa said, staring at the blackened leaves. Luckily the tree was too damp for it to burst into flames.

Since Pippa had pulled back from the nest, the dragonflies seemed to have forgotten about her and were now competing to see who could produce the longest stream of fire. Slowly Pippa edged closer again. All she had to do was grab the horseshoe while the dragonflies were busy playing. But the nest was too hot and there was no way she could reach the horseshoe without getting scorched. Disappointment nearly overwhelmed her. She couldn't go back empty-handed. There had to be a way of retrieving the horseshoe! Pippa racked her brains but her thoughts were tangled like knotted string. Below her the unicorns were still singing. She let her thoughts drift as she tuned into their music. And suddenly she had it – the solution to her problem! Trembling with excitement, she leaned out of the tree.

'Unicorns,' she called down, 'please can you sing me a lullaby?'

The unicorns stopped singing and stared up at Pippa with blank faces.

'A lullaby,' she called again. 'A song for bedtime. Something gentle . . .' She trailed off, feeling unnerved by the unicorns' collective stares.

Then one voice began singing. '*Hush, little dragonfly, stop that fire. Listen to the lullaby and you'll soon tire. Don't breathe flames, close your eyes. Go to sleep, good dragonflies.*'

'That's it, Misty!' Pippa exclaimed in delight.

Misty stopped singing and the tree began to sing back to her in the same soft tone.

'Now everyone join in,' called Pippa. 'Including you, Honey!'

When the tree finished, Misty started again and this time Goldie and Stardust joined in. Honey opened her mouth then flushed and quickly closed it. Stardust nudged her encouragingly. Honey looked uncertain but Stardust kept smiling until, at last, Honey joined in too.

Pippa sent her a huge smile. It was good to see that Honey had overcome her fear of singing in public. The lullaby was making Pippa feel sleepy, but the dragonflies weren't listening. They were having too much fun huffing out streams of fire. Steadfastly Misty, Goldie, Stardust and Honey sang on.

Pippa joined in with them. '*Hush, little dragonfly, stop that fire . . .*'

Was it her imagination or were there more voices singing? Snatching a very

quick look down, she was thrilled to
see that all the unicorns had joined in.
Soon their tuneful voices and the beautiful echo of the tree began to drown
the roars of the baby dragonflies.

'*Listen to the lullaby and you'll soon
tire . . .*' Pippa sang on.

The flames shooting from the nest

were slowing down. The littlest dragonfly was swaying as if she could hardly keep her eyes open. As Pippa watched, she settled down with her head tucked under a pretty pink wing. The purple-winged dragonfly was next. Yawning sleepily, he lay down and within seconds he was snoring. The red dragonfly's head was nodding. Collapsing in the bottom of the nest, she closed her eyes. Only the turquoise dragonfly was left awake, roaring and spitting out red jets of flames. Suddenly he looked round. He seemed surprised to see he was the only baby who still wanted to play. With an indignant snort and one last puff of fire, he snuggled down in the nest.

Straight away Pippa reached for the horseshoe. The dragonfly opened an eye and stared at her.

'Hush,' she whispered, staying very still.

The dragonfly flapped his wings half-heartedly. Then he closed his eyes and fell asleep.

Pippa snatched up the horseshoe, wedged it in her pocket and began the long climb back down the tree.

Chapter 5

As Pippa scrambled back down, Stardust positioned herself under the lowest branch.

'Thank you,' said Pippa. It was such a relief to land on Stardust's back and slide safely to the ground.

'You were brilliant,' Stardust said, nuzzling her nose against Pippa's neck.

'So were you . . .' Pippa trailed

off, conscious that it had gone very quiet.

Misty was staring at her accusingly. 'What have you done to our tree?' she challenged.

'Erm,' Pippa faltered, knowing exactly what Misty meant.

'It's stopped singing! Listen.' Misty hummed a bar of the lullaby and waited, her golden horn pointing at the tree as if inviting it to hum back to her.

The tree remained silent.

'You've hurt our tree,' said Misty.

'No,' Pippa said, pulling the horseshoe out of her pocket. 'It's not my fault. You see, it's because of this horseshoe. It's magic – that's what made the tree sing. But the horseshoe doesn't belong here. We have to return it to the ancient Whispering Wall at Stableside Castle before Midsummer Day or Chevalia will fade away.'

'You didn't say that the tree would stop singing,' Misty replied.

Behind her, the watching unicorns nodded in agreement.

Misty quickly tossed her head. There was a flash of gold and suddenly she was wearing the horseshoe on her horn. A loud cheer rang out and the unicorns stamped their hooves.

Pippa stared at her empty hands and gasped.

'Give that back,' Stardust said, squaring up to Misty. 'The horseshoe doesn't belong here.'

'It does now. We unicorns love our singing tree. We're keeping the horse-shoe.'

Pippa didn't want to upset the unicorns, but she knew she had to get the horseshoe back to the Whispering Wall for their own good, and the good of all Chevalia. She did some quick thinking then went and stood between Stardust and Misty.

'Chevalia is your home too, and if you keep the golden horseshoe then you will lose more than just this tree. The whole Cloud Forest will disappear. That's why you have to give the horseshoe back. But if you love to sing then how about singing with the Royal Ponies? Your voices are so beautiful they could learn from you. You

wouldn't even have to leave the Cloud Forest,' she added hastily, as Misty started to protest. 'We could ask the Royal Court to come here.'

Misty turned her back on Pippa and spoke to her family in urgent whispers. Pippa strained her ears trying to work out what they were saying.

At last, Misty turned back to Pippa and said, 'They don't believe your story about Royal Ponies, a Castle and a wall that whispers. It all sounds like make-believe. They want me to keep the golden horseshoe, but if you bring the ponies of the Royal Court here to sing with us, then they would believe you.'

Pippa hopped on to Stardust's back.

'We'll bring them here straight away,' she promised.

Pippa was very glad that Honey was with them – she'd been to the Cloud Forest many times and had a good idea of which way to go. But even Honey got lost in the immense forest, and twice they had to retrace their hoof steps.

It was lunchtime when they finally returned to the Castle. Pippa's stomach grumbled as they threaded their way through the packed dining room. The rosy red apples piled in the feeding troughs looked delicious. There was no time to stop for food, though. With Stardust and Honey at her side, she made her way to the top of the room, where Queen Moonshine and King Firestar were eating from their golden trough.

Pippa, Stardust and Honey gave low curtsies.

'Your Majesties,' Pippa began, 'we're sorry for interrupting your

lunch but we have something important to ask.'

Queen Moonshine pushed aside a
large carrot. 'Go on, my child,' she said.

The dining room fell silent. Pippa's
ears burned as she quickly explained in
a loud, clear voice what had happened
that morning.

When she'd finished, she heard Cinders snort and whisper loudly to her mother, Baroness Divine, 'She expects us to believe that?'

Several other ponies added exclamations of disbelief. There were whinnies of 'Make-believe!' and lots of laughter.

Pippa's face was hot with anger. 'It's true,' she said, wheeling round to address the dining room. 'Why would I make it up? Come to the Cloud Forest and see for yourselves.' She paused to stare around the room. 'If you're brave enough, that is.'

The laughter turned to mutters. Pippa noticed Divine whispering something in Cinders's ear. Cinders nodded earnestly then she quietly slipped from the room.

Pippa turned to Stardust. 'I'm sorry,' she began. 'I tried my best –'

Someone was banging a hoof for silence. A hush fell as Baroness Divine stood and addressed the dining room.

'I say we give the girl a chance. Maybe she is telling the truth. And if she isn't, well, maybe it's time she left the island.' She stared at Pippa, her square face tilted, her brown eyes challenging.

Pippa stared back. Her heart was thumping so loudly she was amazed that no one else could hear it.

'Thank you, Baroness Divine,' she said.

Divine nodded. 'If Your Majesties agree then I suggest we leave for the Cloud Forest immediately. And if the horseshoe isn't there then Pippa must return to her home.'

Pippa opened her mouth to protest but thought better of it. Divine was baiting her. If she didn't agree to her terms then Divine would accuse her of making the whole story up. But the story was true, and soon she'd be able to prove it.

'Pippa, are you happy to take us to the Cloud Forest?' asked Queen Moonshine.

'Yes, Your Majesty,' Pippa said loudly.

'Then let us depart,' said the Queen.

☆

At first the Royal Ponies chatted noisily and there was lots of laughter as they trotted through the Grasslands and the Savannah. But as the Cloud Forest came into view, the procession slowed and the chatter died away. At the edge of the forest, Pippa, Stardust and Honey waited for everyone else to catch up.

'Are we really going in?' grumbled Princess Cloud. 'Hasn't the joke gone far enough?'

'It's not a joke,' Pippa said quietly.

Even bossy Princess Crystal's eyes were round with fear. Her voice cracked when she asked, 'Does *everyone* have to go in?'

'The unicorns are expecting the entire Royal Court,' Stardust said impatiently. 'But if anyone's too scared to enter then just wait here.'

Many of the ponies were trembling but no one wanted to look like a coward. When Pippa stepped into the forest they all followed. The responsibility weighed heavily on Pippa. Would they be able to find their way back to the unicorns? And would Misty honour her promise to return the golden horseshoe when the Royal Ponies appeared and sang?

Pippa led the procession of ponies through the mist, retracing her steps from the morning's adventure. As the giant tree finally came into sight, Pippa stared up its thick, redwood trunk to the dragonfly nest, from which a fountain of flames could be seen shooting out every now and again. Seeing the tree once more made her appreciate just how high it was, and knowing she had scaled it gave her a burst of courage.

The Royal Ponies stopped a metre from the base of the tree to stare openly at the unicorns. The unicorns stared back in silence. It was hard to say which party was most surprised to see the other. The unicorns and ponies had more in common than they realised and there was no need to be afraid of each other. Then Pippa realised something and her mouth fell open. It wasn't just Honey and Goldie, and Stardust and Misty, who looked alike. The ponies all seemed to have a unicorn double, identical in every way except for their horns and sizes.

Nudging Stardust, Pippa whispered, 'Look – every pony has a unicorn twin.'

Princess Crystal had noticed this too. Soon she was moving around the tree, pairing the ponies up with their unicorn double. When everyone had a partner, Crystal and Petal, her unicorn twin, both raised a hoof and began to conduct.

The unicorns sang first, one line at a time, then waited for the ponies to sing back to them. Their voices complemented each other's so beautifully that the sound was even more wonderful than that of the singing tree. Stardust sang to Misty, Honey to Goldie, and Queen Moonshine to a magnificent unicorn with a tall, golden horn. There were even stocky unicorn equivalents of Cinders and Divine.

'That's so beautiful,' Pippa said, swallowing down a lump in her throat.

As the song ended and the voices faded away, Crystal and Petal bowed to each other.

Queen Moonshine stepped forward, curtsying to her unicorn double, who

was wearing a tiny gold crown decorated with purple daisy-like flowers.

'I'm Moonshine, Queen of Chevalia,' she said. 'That was wonderful. We'd be honoured if you would join us for the Royal Concert on Midsummer Day.'

'I'm Sunrise, Queen of the Cloud Forest.' The unicorn's voice tinkled like a mountain stream. 'It would be our pleasure to host the concert here in the Cloud Forest.'

The sound of hoof beats jarred in Pippa's ears. Turning quickly, she saw two scruffy ponies darting away through the trees. An icy shiver ran down her spine. The ponies running away were Night Mares!

She called urgently to Misty, 'Where's the magical horseshoe?'

'Here,' Misty said, pointing her horn at a fallen log. Her face crumpled in bewilderment. 'Where's it gone? I definitely left it there.'

Pippa noticed Cinders and Divine share a smug smile.

'Divine, have you seen the horse-shoe?' asked Pippa.

'No, I'm afraid not,' Divine replied. 'Are you sure there was a horseshoe here? Or did you just make that up to get attention?'

The watching ponies shifted their hooves as they muttered among themselves.

'It *was* here,' Stardust confirmed. 'Perhaps it fell off the log?'

'No,' Pippa said grimly. 'I've just seen two Night Mares running away through the forest. They must have stolen the horseshoe while we were singing.'

'More make-believe.' Divine tutted.

'Quick,' cried Stardust. 'Jump on

my back, Pippa. We have to catch
them!'

Pippa vaulted on to Stardust's back
and hung on tight to her long, white
mane as the Princess Pony galloped
after the Night Mares.

Chapter 6

A thick mist enveloped Stardust and Pippa as they raced through the Cloud Forest. Pippa stared all around her, ducking frequently to avoid being snagged by low-hanging branches. The Night Mares had the head start but Stardust was fast – and much quicker at turning. She began to gain on them.

'Stop!' shouted Pippa. 'Stop, you thieves!'

In the distance Pippa could hear the roar of the river. If Stardust could reach the stepping stones before the Night Mares there was a good chance they could get the horseshoe back.

'Faster.' She leaned forward, urging Stardust on.

Mud and leaves were kicked up by Stardust's hooves. Her breath came out in snorts and her sides heaved as she chased after the Night Mares. They were almost at the riverbank when she finally caught up with them. As she stopped, Pippa leapt from her back and ran towards the biggest of the scruffy ponies, who was carrying the golden horseshoe in his mouth. His forelegs were in the water but he was hesitating.

'Which stone do I tread on first? Lightning, can you remember?'

'Um,' Lightning said, stretching out a hoof then quickly pulling it back. 'Are you sure we crossed here, Thunder? The river's very fast-flowing.'

'Useless brother! Of course it was here,' roared Thunder. 'Why did the Mistress pair me with you for such an important mission?'

'Take that back. I'm not useless – I spotted the horseshoe,' Lightning said, blocking Thunder's path.

'Get out of the way,' Thunder growled, shoving past him.

'No!' Lightning whinnied in fright as he slipped on the muddy bank and fell, taking Thunder down with him.

There was a loud splash as the Night Mares landed in the river. The two brothers struggled to their hooves, their dark manes plastered to their faces. Pippa and Stardust roared with laughter as Thunder and Lightning splashed around. But the current was too strong and suddenly they lost their balance and were swept away downstream. Pippa and Stardust stopped laughing then.

'We have to help them,' cried Pippa.

'And save the horseshoe,' Stardust added.

They hurried along the bank after the Night Mares. Willowy trees grew alongside the river and their long branches trailed in the water.

'Grab the branches!' Pippa called. She didn't want the thieves to escape with the horseshoe but she certainly didn't want them to drown.

The Night Mares listened to Pippa and swam to the opposite bank, where, grabbing on to the branches, they pulled themselves out of the rushing water.

Pippa and Stardust stopped and stared at them in dismay. Still clinging on to the willowy branches, the Night Mares stood in the shallows while they regained their breath.

'You can't catch us now,' Lightning shouted triumphantly.

Pippa heard hooves bounding up behind her. Misty dashed past, stopping at the water's edge. She leaned down, dipped her horn in the water then quickly stood up. Pippa's ears rang with a cracking sound as the river began to freeze over.

'What's happening?' she yelled over the creaks and groans of the water turning to ice.

'It's horn magic,' Misty explained. 'All unicorns have a magic horn and they can do one special thing with it. My horn freezes water and melts it again.'

Soon the river was a thick slab of smooth ice. The Night Mares were having trouble standing and leaned against each other for support. Thunder tried to climb on to the riverbank and lost his footing. He dropped the horseshoe and it skidded across the ice into the middle of the frozen river. Each time he tried to go after it his hooves slid in different directions.

Pippa took off towards the nearest tree. She shinned up it and climbed on

to a willowy branch that was threaded
with vines.

'Careful,' shouted Stardust.

Pippa's heart raced as she grabbed a
vine and swung on it like a rope. When
she swung out over the river she reached
down for the horseshoe. Her fingers
brushed the cold metal but, before she
could pick it up, the vine swung her away
out of reach. Pippa pushed herself back
over the river. Gritting her teeth, she
stretched as far as she could. Her fingers
touched the horseshoe and curled round
it. She quickly snatched it up.

'Hurrah!' Stardust and Misty cheered
as she swung back to the tree.

Misty dipped her head and touched
the frozen river with her horn. With a

groan, the ice split down the middle and started to melt. Muttering and grumbling, the Night Mares waded through the slushy ice, climbed on to the opposite bank and trotted away, their heads low.

Pippa threw her arms around Stardust and hugged her tight.

'We did it!'

Misty hung back, until Pippa put out an arm and drew her close. They were still hugging when a voice echoed behind them.

'Well done, everyone.'

Pippa turned round to see Queen Moonshine leading the ponies and unicorns through the trees towards them.

She nuzzled Pippa's curly, brown hair with her nose. 'You've been very brave. We should never have doubted you.'

'Stardust and Misty were very brave too,' Pippa said quickly.

'Yes, they were,' Queen Moonshine agreed. 'And now it's time to return to the Castle. We must hang this fifth horseshoe back on the wall where it belongs before anything else happens to it.' She turned to address the unicorns. 'Please would you all grant me the honour of joining us? We'd love you to stay with us and sing at our special Midsummer concert.'

The unicorns shuffled awkwardly, until Misty stepped forward.

'Thank you. That would be a great

honour for us too, but . . .' she hesitated, 'we're unable to leave the Cloud Forest.'

'Why?' Stardust blurted out, unable to hide her disappointment.

Misty still hesitated, a pink flush creeping over her face. 'We've never left the forest before – we're too scared to. We know about the ghosts who live beyond the trees.'

Pippa bit the inside of her lip to stop a smile. 'We thought there were ghosts in the Cloud Forest until we met you, but there's no such thing.' She pushed a damp curl of hair out of her face. 'And even if you are scared, you shouldn't let it stop you doing the things you want to. I was terrified when I climbed the tree and faced the baby dragonflies. Honey was scared when we all sang the lullaby together. The Royal Ponies were frightened to come into the Cloud Forest. But we all managed to conquer our fears.'

'Please come,' said Stardust. 'Your voices are wonderful. It would be amazing if we could all sing together at the ancient Whispering Wall on Midsummer Day.'

Misty looked thoughtful.

'I'll come if I can sing a duet with Honey?' Goldie spoke up.

Honey shook her head sadly. 'I'm sorry but my voice isn't good enough for that.'

'It would be if you practised – and I can help you,' replied Goldie.

'That's very brave of you,' said Misty.

Honey pawed the ground. She took a deep breath and quickly said, 'OK, I'll do it.'

Misty touched her horn to Honey's, then she gracefully spun round to face the watching unicorns.

'These ponies have shown such courage by coming here today. And now Honey has shown even more bravery by agreeing to sing a duet with Goldie. Can you overcome your fears too?'

There were bright flashes of sunlight sparkling on golden horns as every

single unicorn dipped his or her head in
agreement.

'Yes,' they chorused, their voices
chiming like magical bells.

Misty nodded back at them proudly.
'Let's go to the Castle,' she said with a
smile.

The late afternoon air seemed to shimmer with the beautiful voices as unicorns and ponies stood together and practised their singing before the Whispering Wall. Sun streamed into the courtyard, its long, glittering fingers brushing the four golden horseshoes already hanging on the wall, making them sparkle and glitter with magic.

As the voices soared, Pippa stepped forward and hung the fifth horseshoe on Misty. Her fingers tingled with magic as the golden horseshoe met the golden horn. There was a brilliant flash of light and Pippa shielded her eyes with her hands. Misty stood up on her back hooves and placed the horseshoe on an empty black nail.

Pippa's smile was so wide she thought her face might split in two.

'Five horseshoes safe,' she whispered to Stardust.

'Five,' Stardust echoed happily. 'There are only three left to find now. We're going to do this, aren't we?'

Midsummer was in two days' time.

Doubt stole through Pippa like an icy breeze. Could they really find all the horseshoes by then?

The unicorns and ponies finished their song and started a new one. Their voices swelled in the air, carrying Pippa's doubts away.

She nodded her head. 'Yes!' she said confidently. 'Yes, we are.'

Chevalia Now!

EXCLUSIVE INTERVIEW WITH PRINCESS HONEY

By Tulip Inkhoof

Chevalia's Cloud Forest has long been thought to be haunted by ghosts. But today two brave ponies and one brave girl ventured into the mysterious forest and revealed its special secret: unicorns live there!

This reporter caught up with Princess Honey, who's been visiting her unicorn friend, Goldie, in the Cloud Forest ever since she was a young foal.

☆ **TI (Tulip Inkhoof):** Honey, how did you discover the secretive unicorns?

☆ **H (Honey):** First of all can I just say that I *love* your purple hoof polish. It's so sparkly!

☆ **TI:** Oh, thank you – I visited the Mane Street Salon on my way to Stableside Castle.

☆ **H:** I love getting my hooves painted!

☆ **TI:** Me too! But let's talk about the unicorns. How did you find out about them?

☆ **H:** Right, down to business! Well, one day my class at Canter's Prep School went on a trip to the Savannah and I thought I could hear singing coming from the nearby Cloud Forest. As I trotted to the edge of the forest, I heard the loveliest songs floating out of it. I knew the legends about the forest but these voices were so beautiful I didn't think they could possibly be ghosts, so I sneaked off and set hoof into the forest.

☆ **TI:** But weren't you frightened?

☆ **H:** Oh, I was, and I thought about turning around. Instead I sang back. I repeated the lovely song as I went into the mist – and I came face to face with a small unicorn!

3

☆ **Tl:** How extraordinary!

☆ **H:** Mum and Dad used to tell us unicorn stories at bedtime and I never thought they were real. But this unicorn was definitely real! She introduced herself as Goldie, and do you know what?

☆ **Tl:** What?

☆ **H:** She looks a lot like me!

☆ **Tl:** So you can confirm the rumour about the unicorn twins?

☆ **H:** Yes, all of the ponies on Chevalia have a unicorn that looks like them in the Cloud Forest. Even you, Tulip! It's a very special bond.

☆ **Tl:** I wonder if my unicorn is an enterprising

young reporter?

☆ **H:** Maybe! That first day in the forest I met the unicorn twins for my entire family but as the unicorns were so shy I promised them I wouldn't reveal their secret. Every once in a while, especially if I was feeling low or if the salon couldn't fit me in for a hoof scrub, I'd trot up to the Cloud Forest for a unicorn adventure.

☆ **TI:** So what happened to make you bring Stardust and Pippa with you today?

☆ **H:** I was upset because Stardust was making fun of my singing so I ran away to the Cloud Forest and Stardust and Pippa followed without me realising. Pippa thought that if everyone was scared of the forest then that might make it a good

5

hiding place for the golden horseshoes – and it turned out she was right!

☆ **TI:** I hear that Pippa rescued a horseshoe from a dragonfly nest and then it was nearly stolen by two Night Mares who go by the names of Thunder and Lightning?

☆ **H:** Yes, the Night Mares were crossing the river to get away from us but Misty saved the day with her magical horn by making the river freeze over.

☆ **TI:** What an eventful day! Well, I should let you get back to singing practice.

☆ **H:** Yes, Goldie and I need to practise our duet for the Midsummer concert! See you there!

ROYAL CONCERT IN DANGER

By Tulip Inkhoof

Breaking news!

Despite finding five of the eight missing horseshoes and welcoming the unicorns to rehearse with the Royal Family, Princess Crystal has just confirmed that the Royal Concert won't go ahead unless all eight horseshoes are back on the Whispering Wall in time.

☆ 'Stableside Castle won't hold the traditional concert if the horseshoes aren't returned safely by Midsummer Day,'

8

she read from a prepared statement outside the Castle gates. As the ponarazzi snapped photos of the eldest Princess Pony, looking very much the Queen-in-waiting, Crystal refused to answer questions from the press.

☆ But this plucky reporter has learnt that while the Castle is trying to appear calm, inside the Castle walls the Royal Family is growing increasingly anxious about the coming sundown on Midsummer Day.

☆ There's no denying that something strange is going on. Every single time our intrepid duo of Princess Stardust and Pippa get close to the missing horseshoes, the Night Mares seem to be one hoof ahead. They keep springing from nowhere, snatching the horseshoes from our heroines.

☆ Very little is known about the Night Mares, and until this week most ponies considered them nothing more than characters in spooky stories. Yet with the discovery of real unicorns in the misty mountainside and reports of the Night Mares' involvement in the mystery, there may be more truth to the rumours than any pony is letting on.

☆ **All eyes are on the human girl, Pippa MacDonald, sent from the human world to help save Chevalia. Can she do it? This reporter thinks she can – this reporter hopes she can.**